# The Best Mother's Day Ever

by Eleanor May
illustrated by MH Pilz

Kane Press, Inc.
New York

For my mother and my daughter—E.M.

For my Mom—MHP

Acknowledgments: Our thanks to Alma B. Ramírez for helping us make this book as accurate as possible.

Text copyright © 2010 by Eleanor May
Illustrations copyright © 2010 by MH Pilz

Library of Congress Cataloging-in-Publication Data

May, Eleanor.
  The best Mother's Day ever / by Eleanor May ; illustrated by MH Pilz.
    p. cm. — (Social studies connects)
  Summary: Lucy wants to make Mother's Day special, avoiding the disasters she usually creates, so she works with her neighbor, Diego, to celebrate the holiday as it is done in Mexico.
  ISBN 978-1-57565-299-3 (pbk. : alk. paper)
  [1. Mother's Day—Fiction. 2. Mexican Americans—Fiction. 3. Holidays—Mexico—Fiction.]
  I. Pilz, MH, ill. II. Title.
  PZ7.M4513Bes 2010
  [E]—dc22
                                    2009024489


10 9 8 7 6 5 4 3 2 1

First published in the United States of America in 2010 by Kane Press, Inc.
Printed in Hong Kong.

Book Design: Edward Miller

Social Studies Connects is a registered trademark of Kane Press, Inc.

**www.kanepress.com**

I sit back on my heels and look at my card. Hmm. Does it need more glitter? Or maybe a giant heart around *I Love You, Mom*?

Mother's Day is tomorrow. And I really, really want it to be great—for once.

It's not that I haven't tried. Like
last year. How was I supposed to
know there was a bee inside
that bunch of flowers I picked?

Or the year before. Making waffles with the E-Z
Waffle Maker turned out to be H-A-R-D.
 Mom always says it's the thought that counts.
But she only tells me that when I mess up.

"Wow!" Diego says. "Your card is *awful,* Lucy!"

Diego lives next door. When he moved here from Mexico last year, he spoke hardly any English. Now he speaks it well—except for a few mix-ups.

"Um . . . you mean 'awesome,' right?" I ask.

"Awesome." He smiles. *"Claro."*

*Claro* is Spanish for "of course."

When people move to America, they bring something that can't fit in a suitcase—their culture or way of life. Language, beliefs, music, foods, and art are all part of a person's culture.

Diego says holidays are different in Mexico. Instead of Halloween, they celebrate the Day of the Dead. And they have their Independence Day in September, not July.

"What do you have in Mexico instead of Mother's Day?" I ask Diego.

He laughs. "We have Mother's Day too."

On Mexico's Day of the Dead, two days after Halloween, people honor friends and family who have died. They remember happy stories about them, make their favorite meals, and bring sugar skulls and marigolds to their graves.

Diego tells me about Mother's Day in the town where he used to live. "Very early, before sunrise, all the kids wake up their mothers with a special morning song."

"Really?" I picture my mom in the morning. "Do they like getting woken up so early?"

"*Claro!* Then we cook a special breakfast—"

"We do that too!" I say. "Breakfast in bed."

Diego looks confused. "You cook in the bed?"

I laugh. "No, you cook it in the kitchen. Then you take it to your mom in bed."

"But why?"

I think about it. Then I shrug. "I don't know. But it makes mothers happy."

Later, at home, I think more about Mother's Day. Talking to Diego has given me an idea.

My mom loves stuff from other countries. Movies. Music. Food.

What if I give her a Mexican Mother's Day?

Lucy's mom does Chinese exercises, collects Russian dolls, and has masks from Africa on her wall. Look around your house and you'll probably find things from other countries too!

When you greet a friend in America, you might say "Hi." In France you might kiss your friend—on both cheeks. In Japan you might bow. But no matter how we do it, we're all happy to greet our friends!

I call out my window and tell Diego my idea. "Can you teach me the morning song?" I ask.

"*Claro!*" he says. "And you can help me make breakfast on bed."

I run over to Diego's.

He sings me the song. And sings. And sings.
It's pretty, but it's long.

Now I know why they start singing so early.
To get done in time for breakfast!

There are more than 6,000 different languages used in the world. And in every language, people love to sing songs!

We practice the Spanish words.

"I'll never learn all this by tomorrow," I moan.

"You could sing an English song instead," Diego suggests.

That makes sense. But the only songs I know are camp songs. "Greasy Grimy Gopher Guts" doesn't seem right for Mother's Day.

Before I go home, we try out Diego's new video game, *Rockin' Soccer II*. But I can't seem to keep my mind on it.

I want this to be the best Mother's Day ever. Just once, I don't want to hear my mom say it's the thought that counts.

Soccer is the most popular sport in Mexico—and in lots of other countries, too. In many places, the soccer World Cup is the year's biggest sporting event—way bigger than the Super Bowl or the World Series in the U.S.!

After dinner Mom blasts her favorite CD and
we dance around. She really likes this song.
I wish I could sing it to her tomorrow. But the
only words I can make out are "baby, baby."

Then it hits me. Who says I have to *sing*?

It'll still be a Mexican Mother's Day. Kind of.
I'll just do it my way.

I'm so jazzed, I'm sure I won't sleep a wink.
But before I know it, my alarm clock buzzes.
Four A.M.

I rub my eyes and yawn. It's Mother's Day!
Time to help Diego make breakfast in bed!

Diego is already in his kitchen.

"So, what does your mom like?" I whisper.
"Scrambled eggs? Toast? Orange juice?"

"Tamales," Diego says.

"Tamales? For breakfast?"

*"Claro!"* he says.

In different countries, people eat different foods. Sometimes the *way* they eat is different, too. They might use chopsticks, or eat with their fingers, or only eat with their right hands.

We mix the dough for the tamales. It's a lot like making cookies.

I scoop dough onto each corn husk, and we put some veggies and cheese on top.

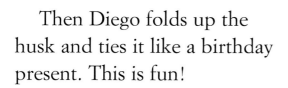

Then Diego folds up the husk and ties it like a birthday present. This is fun!

Diego takes out a pot and fills it with tamales. He pours in a little water and puts the pot on the stove.

"Now what?" I ask.

Diego smiles. "Now we wait for them to cook."

Americans eat everything from tamales (Mexico) to pizza (Italy) to sushi (Japan)— thanks to all the people who moved here and brought their recipes along!

While we're waiting, we play *Rockin' Soccer* with the sound off. Yummy smells float in from the kitchen.

I look out the window. It's not so dark now. If we want to wake my mom up before sunrise, we'd better get moving!

We slip in the back door. I grab Mom's boombox. Her favorite CD is still inside.

Diego looks a little worried. "Are you sure your mom will like this?"

"*Claro!*" I say.

We tiptoe up the stairs and push open her
bedroom door.

I plug in the boombox, flip the power switch,
and turn the volume up as high as it will go. Then
I press PLAY.

STOP    PLAY

I flip on the light.
Uh-oh.
Diego yanks the plug.
"Um . . ." I say. "Happy Mother's Day?"
Mom points at us. "OUT. NOW."

I trail Diego down the stairs. He stops short. "What's that noise?"

I listen. It sounds like a—

"Smoke alarm!" I say. "And it's coming from your house!"

We stare at each other. The tamales!

Before we reach his door, it flies open. Diego's
father comes out carrying our pot. Smoke curls
out of the top.

We peek in.

I don't know much about making tamales. But
I am pretty sure they're not supposed to smell
like that.

While Diego and I try to explain to his father, our mothers come into the yard. They do not look happy.

I gulp. Maybe this would be a good time to go get those Mother's Day cards.

Diego slumps into a chair. "This is awesome,"
he groans.

I know what he means.

All I wanted was a Mother's Day where Mom
would not say, "It's the thought that counts."
I think I got my wish. Seeing how mad she is,
that's the last thing she'll say!

But when our parents come inside together, they are laughing!

"A sunrise song," my mom says. "With a boombox."

Diego's father shakes his head. "Kids. Anywhere you go, they are the same."

They all laugh again.

Our parents make us promise to get help the next time we try cooking tamales. Then Diego and I give our moms the cards we made.

"It's beautiful!" Mom says, and hugs me.

Diego's mother says, *"Qué bonita!"*

Mother's Day is celebrated in more than fifty countries around the world. In Sweden money is raised for poor mothers. In Japan kids draw pictures of "My Mother" and enter them in a contest!

"I wanted to have a special Mother's Day,"
I say. "But it didn't turn out quite the way we
hoped."

Diego's mother smiles and pats my shoulder.
"In Mexico, we say, *La intención es lo que cuenta.*"

"What does that mean?" I ask.

Diego says, "It's the thought that counts."

Diego and I look at each other and laugh.
"Mothers," I say. "I guess anywhere you go,
they are the same!"

People may eat tamales or
turkey burgers. They may
say "mother" or "madre"
or "mère" or "majii." But
whatever our differences,
deep down we are a lot alike!

We understand similarities and differences!

# MAKING CONNECTIONS

Things can be similar and different at the same time! For example, one flower might be purple and another flower might be blue—but maybe they both have five petals. It's the same with people! Think about it. Kids from all parts of the world share many similarities and differences. What are some ways you might be like a kid who seems different from you or who lives far away?

## Look Back
• Look at Lucy's and Diego's cards on page 3. How are the cards similar? How are they different?
• On pages 6–8, what do you learn about Mother's Day in Mexico? How is it like or unlike Mother's Day in the U.S.?

## Try This!
Look at each set of pictures. What's similar and what's different about the flags? How about the kids?

Set 1:

**U.S. FLAG**          **AUSTRALIAN FLAG**

Set 2: